Katherine Tegen Books is an imprint of HarperCollins Publishers.

A Creature Was Stirring
Text copyright © 2023 by Heather S. Pierczynski
Illustrations copyright © 2023 by Skylar Hogan
All rights reserved. Manufactured in Italy.
No part of this book may be used or reproduced in any manner whatsoever without written permission
except in the case of brief quotations embodied in critical articles and reviews. For information address
HarperCollins Children's Books, a division of HarperCollins Publishers, 195 Broadway, New York, NY 10007.
www.harpercollinschildrens.com

ISBN 978-0-06-323074-3

The artist used an iPad Pro and Procreate to create the digital illustrations for this book.
Typography by Molly Fehr
23 24 25 26 27 RTLO 10 9 8 7 6 5 4 3 2 1
First Edition

A Creature Was Stirring

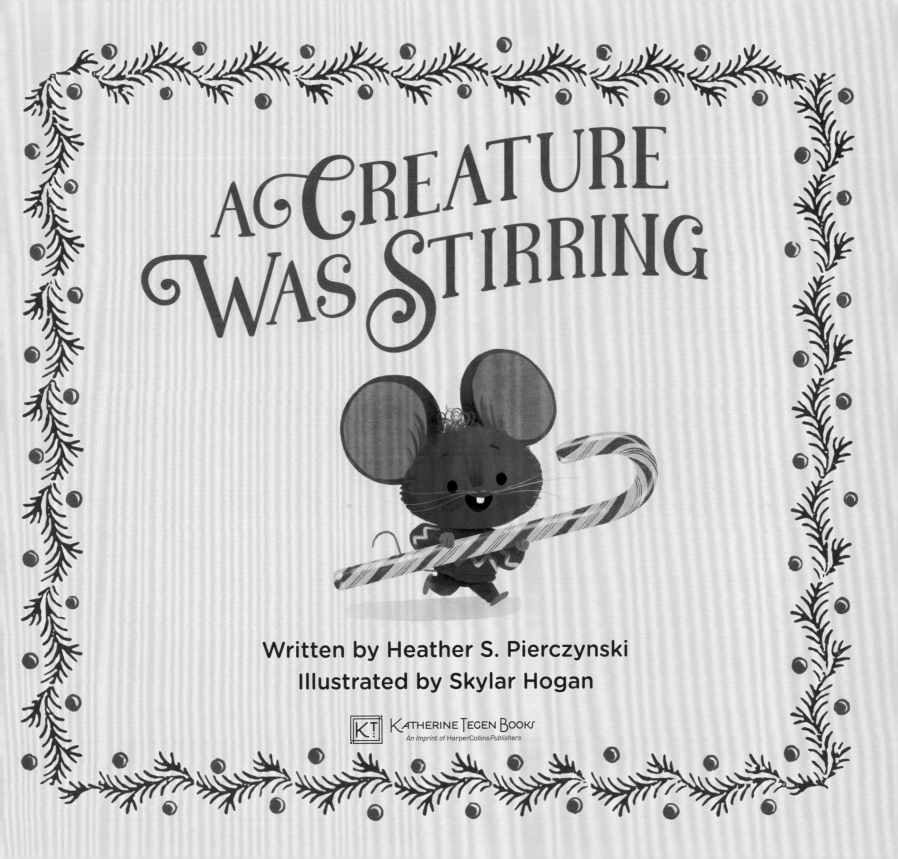

Written by Heather S. Pierczynski

Illustrated by Skylar Hogan

KT KATHERINE TEGEN BOOKS
An Imprint of HarperCollins Publishers

'Twas the night before Christmas,
when all through the house,
not a creature was stirring, not even a—

MOUSE!

He'd never heard of a mouse *not stirring*.
And tonight was his favorite night of the year.

So . . .

He stirred.

Squeaked.

Eeked!

And jangled the cat's jingle bells.

"Go to bed," whispered the cat.
"It's the night before Christmas."

But Mouse was too excited.
And he'd never heard of a
mouse *not stirring*.

So he drummed.

Stacked.

Nut-cracked.

And crunched on all the cookies.

"Go to bed," warned the *other* cat. "It's the night before Christmas."

But Mouse could not wait until morning. And he'd never heard of a mouse *not stirring*.

So he smooched.

Buzzed.

Boinged.

And tricycled around the tree.

Then he guzzled.

Caroled.

Snowplowed.

And paraded down the street.

"GO TO BED, MOUSE!"
roared the house

and the neighborhood

and the city

and the world.

"IT'S THE
NIGHT BEFORE
CHRISTMAS."

"Okay, okay," Mouse said.

So he went to bed.

But he could not fall asleep.

He twiddled.

Fiddled.

Giggled.

And wondered how all the other creatures could fall asleep on the most glorious night of the year.

Then Mouse threw down
his covers.

Jumped on his sled.

Dashed down the stairway.

And hopped the train
at full steam ahead.

HUFF and PUFF
and CHUG and CHUG
and "MERRY CHOO-CHOO!"

HUFF and PUFF
and CHUG and CHUG
and "MERRY CHRISTMAS!"

HUFF and PUFF and CHUG and
CHUG and "UP THE CHIMNEY!"

HUFF and PUFF and
CHUG and CHUG and—

"DON'T CRASH INTO ME!"

shouted Santa.

But the train was much too fast. So when Mouse *accidentally* hit the gas, it REVVed—
VROOMed!
SCREECHed!

KABOOMed!

Straight into Santa—
and every toy in his sack.

"Oh dear," said Santa. "I think you'd better open your present now."

Mouse untied the ribbon and took a quiet, curious look. There in the box he found a tiny little book.

He opened its shiny cover and squealed at the story ahead. He turned to the first page and twirled his whiskers while he read.

"'Twas the night before Christmas, when all through the house, not a creature was stirring, not even a—"

"—MOUSE?! ME? OH NO, I'VE RUINED CHRISTMAS!" he cried.

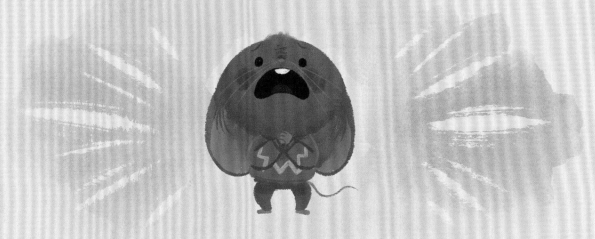

"Shhhhhhh!" Santa whispered.
"You did not ruin Christmas,
but maybe you should just . . ."

"Go to bed now?"
Mouse asked.

"Exactly," Santa said.

So Mouse eased back into the station.

And slipped just past the cats.

And tiptoed up the stairway . . .

into his bed at last.

And as he snuggled under the covers,
he spied the sleigh and reindeer in flight.
And just when he fell asleep reading . . .

Santa called, "To all a very good night."

And finally, on the night before Christmas, and all through the house, not a creature was stirring, not even a—

To Henry, may you never stop stirring. —H.S.P.

For Buom and Mal, my favorite noisy creatures. —S.H.